𝒟𝒾𝓈𝓃𝑒𝓎 · **Pocket Classics**

The Princess Collection

First published in the UK in 2024 by Studio Press,
an imprint of Bonnier Books UK,
4th Floor, Victoria House, Bloomsbury Square, London WC1B 4DA
Owned by Bonnier Books,
Sveavägen 56, Stockholm, Sweden

www.bonnierbooks.co.uk

Printed in China
2 4 6 8 10 9 7 5 3 1

All rights reserved
ISBN 978-1-80078-954-8

Edited by Frankie Jones
Designed by Maddox Philpot
Production by Giulia Caparrelli

DISNEY ✦ **Pocket Classics**

The Princess Collection

Snow White ✦ Sleeping Beauty ✦ Cinderella

STUDIO PRESS

Walt Disney's
Snow White
and the SEVEN DWARFS

Cover illustration by Don Williams

Long ago, in a faraway kingdom, there lived a lovely young princess named Snow White.

Soon she was Princess of the land. And she and her husband, the charming Prince, rode to their palace in a golden coach to live happily ever after!

The Grand Duke was about to leave when Cinderella
came flying down the stairs.

"Oh, wait, wait, please!" she called. "May I try the
slipper on?"

"Of course," said the Duke. But the wicked Stepmother
tripped the servant with the slipper. Crash! It splintered
into a thousand pieces.

"Never mind," said Cinderella. "I have the
other here." And she pulled from her pocket the
other glass slipper!

The household was in a flurry. The Grand Duke and his servant had arrived with the glass slipper.

Each stepsister tried to force her foot into the tiny glass slipper. But they failed.

Meanwhile, the mice made themselves into a long, live chain. The mouse at the end dropped down into the Stepmother's pocket. He popped up again with the key to Cinderella's room!

"The Prince's bride!" whispered Cinderella. "I must dress, too. The Duke must not find me like this."

Cinderella went off to her room, humming a waltzing tune. Then the Stepmother suspected the truth – that Cinderella was the girl the Prince was seeking. So the Stepmother locked her in her room!

"Please let me out – oh, please!" Cinderella cried. But the wicked Stepmother only laughed and went away.

"We will save you!" said the loyal mice.
"We will somehow get that key!"

The next morning, the King learned that the Prince wanted to marry the slipper's owner.

"Find her! Scour the kingdom, but find that girl!" he shouted to the Duke.

News of the Duke's search ran on ahead, and the Stepmother dressed her ugly daughters, hoping that one of them would be the Prince's bride.

She leaped into her coach and raced for home.
But the spell was soon broken.

"Glass slipper!" the mice cried. "Glass slipper!"

Cinderella looked down. Sure enough, there
was a glass slipper on the pavement.

"Oh, thank you, Godmother!" she said.

The Prince and Cinderella danced every dance until the clock in the palace tower began to strike midnight. *Bong! Bong!*

"Oh!" cried Cinderella. The magic was about to end!

Without a word she ran out the door. One of her little glass slippers fell off, but she could not stop.

The King motioned to the musicians, and they struck up a dreamy waltz. The Prince and Cinderella swirled across the dance floor. And the King went happily off to bed.

The Prince's ball was under way. As soon as Cinderella appeared in the doorway, the Prince walked over and asked her to dance.

"There," said the Fairy Godmother. "Now hop in, child. The magic only lasts till midnight!"

"But my dress—" Cinderella looked at her rags.

"Of course you can't go in that!" laughed the Fairy Godmother.

The wand waved again, and there stood Cinderella – in the most beautiful gown in the world, and tiny slippers of glass.

"Let's see now, the first thing you will need is – a pumpkin!"
the Fairy Godmother said.

Cinderella was confused, but she brought over a pumpkin.

The Fairy Godmother said some magic words.

Slowly, the pumpkin turned into a fancy coach.

"What we need next are some fine, big – mice!"

At the touch of the wand Cinderella's little friends
turned into handsome horses.

Then the old horse became a fine coachman.

And Bruno the dog turned into a footman.

Poor Cinderella! She ran to the garden and wept as if
her heart would break.

But soon she felt someone beside her. She looked up,
and through her tears she saw a sweet-faced little woman.
"Oh," said Cinderella. "Good evening. Who are you?"

"I am your Fairy Godmother," said the woman. "Now
dry your tears. You can't go to the ball looking like that!"

"Wait!" cried Cinderella. "I am coming, too!"

The Stepmother and her daughters all turned at the sound of Cinderella's voice.

"My beads!" cried one stepsister.

"And my ribbon!" cried the other. "And those bows! You thief! Those are mine!"

So they ripped and they tore at the dress until Cinderella was in rags once more. And then they pranced off to the ball.

Poor Cinderella!

But when she got to her room, she saw that her little friends had not forgotten her. They had been gathering discarded items from the stepsisters' rooms to fix a party dress for her.

"Oh, how lovely!" she cried. She looked out the window. The coach was still there. So she started to dress for the ball.

Cinderella worked all day long. She did not have a moment to fix herself up, or to give thought to a dress.

"Why, Cinderella, you are not ready," said her Stepmother when the coach was at the door. "What a shame!"

There was much excitement when the invitation to the King's ball came.

"How delightful!" the stepsisters said. "We are going to the palace to a ball!"

"And I," said Cinderella, "I am invited, too!"

"Yes, you!" mocked the Stepmother. "Of course you may go, if you finish your work," she said. "And if you have something suitable to wear. I said *if*."

Now, across the town was the palace of the King. And one day the King himself was giving orders to the Great Grand Duke. "The Prince must marry!" said the King. "It is high time!"

"But first he must fall in love," said the Duke.

"We can arrange that," said the King. "We shall give a great ball this very night and invite every girl in the land!"

Up the long stairway she carried breakfast trays for her Stepmother and her two lazy stepsisters. And down she came with a basket of mending, some clothes to wash, and a long list of jobs to do for the day.

"Now let me see," her Stepmother would say. "You can clean the large carpet in the main hall. And wash all the windows, upstairs and down. Scrub the terrace. Sweep the stairs – and then you may rest."

Every morning, Cinderella woke from her dreams and
went right to work. Out back she set a bowl of milk for the
Stepmother's disagreeable cat, who watched for his chance
to catch the mice. She fed grain to the chickens and ducks
and geese. And Cinderella gave some grain to the mice –
when they were out of reach of the cat, of course. Then
back into the house she went.

But Cinderella was not sad. She made friends with the birds who flew to her windowsill. And her best friends of all were – guess who – the mice!

The mice lived in the attic with Cinderella. She made little clothes for them and gave them all names. And they thought Cinderella was the sweetest girl in the world.

But alas! The kindly gentleman soon died. And his second wife was harsh and cold to her lovely stepdaughter. She cared only for her two ugly daughters.

Everyone called the stepdaughter Cinderella now since she sat by the cinders to keep warm as she worked hard, dressed only in rags.

Once upon a time, there lived a kindly gentleman.
He had a fine home and a lovely daughter, and he gave
her all that money could buy – a pony, a puppy named
Bruno and many beautiful dresses.

But the little girl wished for a mother and for other
children to play with. So her father married a woman
with two daughters of her own. Now, he thought, his
daughter had everything to make her happy.

WALT DISNEY'S
Cinderella

Story adapted by Jane Werner

Illustrated by Retta Scott Worcester

Digital scanning and restoration services
provided by Tim Lewis of Disney Publishing
Worldwide and Ron Stark of S/R Labs

Soon, the palace was buzzing with news of Princess Aurora and Prince Phillip. The king and queen ordered a royal feast in the royal banquet hall. And the festivities continued in the magnificent ballroom, where everyone made merry with music and dancing and laughter. The three good fairies were most joyous of all, for they knew Sleeping Beauty had found true love. The prince and princess danced the night away and lived happily forevermore.

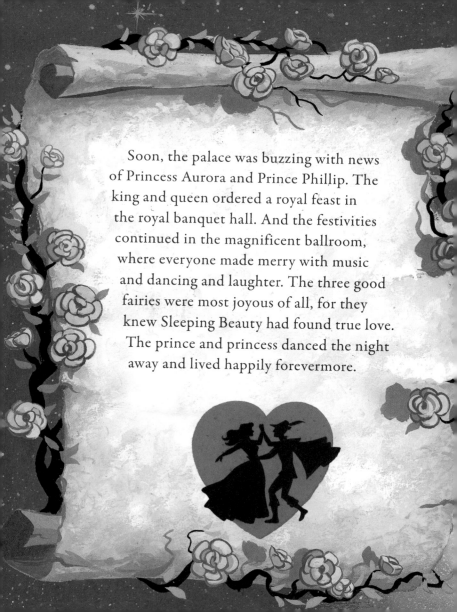

Then, the spell lifted. Yawning and stretching sounds could be heard throughout the entire castle. The king and queen and everyone else slowly woke from their slumber.

The prince dashed to Aurora's side and
gave her the kiss of true love. The princess
began to stir. She fluttered her eyelids open
and awoke at last! Happiness filled her heart
when she saw her handsome prince.

He stumbled back and nearly fell off the cliff.
But the brave prince used his shield and hurled his
mighty sword deep into the heart of the dragon. The
monstrous Maleficent dropped dead, once and for all!

As soon as the prince got to the palace, a fierce and furious dragon appeared before him. It was Maleficent, who used all her powers to transform herself into a fire-breathing dragon! The dragon blasted Phillip with a fiery blaze.

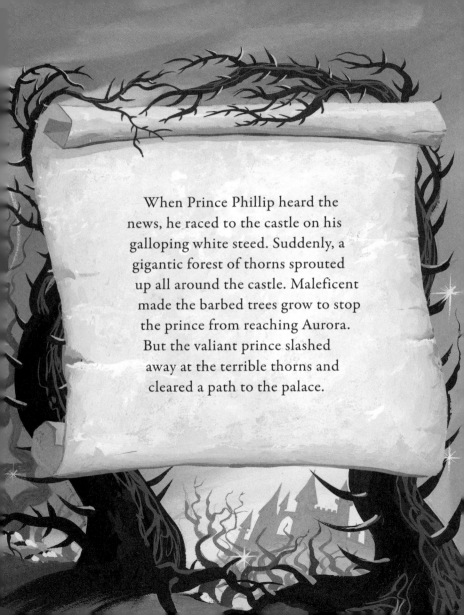

When Prince Phillip heard the
news, he raced to the castle on his
galloping white steed. Suddenly, a
gigantic forest of thorns sprouted
up all around the castle. Maleficent
made the barbed trees grow to stop
the prince from reaching Aurora.
But the valiant prince slashed
away at the terrible thorns and
cleared a path to the palace.

Once the palace was totally quiet, the
fairies flew away with magical speed. They
needed to find the handsome prince who
would break the spell.

Flora, Fauna and Merryweather couldn't bear
to break the king's heart with the news of Aurora's
fate. So they made everyone else in the castle sleep,
too . . . all the guards, the ladies-in-waiting, even
the king and queen.

The princess fell to the floor. The fairies wept, for they couldn't stop Maleficent. But Aurora didn't die. The good fairies worked their magic so that the princess simply fell into a deep sleep. She would awaken only after the first kiss of her true love.

The fairies brought Aurora back
to the castle on the evening of her
sixteenth birthday. Everyone at the
palace eagerly awaited her return.
But the wicked Maleficent also
came to the castle and waited for
the princess. She lured Aurora to
the top of a tower where she saw
a magic spinning wheel. Then,
Maleficent's horrible curse came
to be . . . the princess touched the
spindle and pricked her finger.

Fauna's cake rose to perfection with pink icing and brilliant candles. And Flora's fabric gathered itself, trimmed itself and sewed itself together. In the blink of an eye, it became the finest gown a princess could dream to wear.

Merryweather finally had enough of Flora and Fauna's nonsense. After sixteen years, it was time to get out their wands! They needed magic to clean up their mess! So, with a few simple whisks of their wands . . .

And Flora had never before made a dress. She snipped and clipped here and pinned and patched there, but she only succeeded in making Merryweather cry. Flora had stitched together a gown absolutely unfit for a princess.

Poor Fauna didn't know the first thing about making a cake. She tried and tried and tried, but the only thing she could make was a gooey mess.

Flora wanted to make an extra-special dress. She used Merryweather as a model. First, Flora cut a hole in the center of the cloth for Aurora's feet to go through!

Meanwhile, the fairies were planning a secret birthday surprise. Fauna tried to whip up a fancy layer cake. She simply opened a recipe book and started mixing all the ingredients in a big bowl.

On Princess Aurora's
sixteenth birthday, her dreams
came true! Prince Phillip heard
a beautiful song in the forest
and followed the sound. He
came upon Aurora singing, and
they fell in love at first sight. All
Aurora's forest friends shared
in their joy as the happy couple
danced and danced.

But the princess was never lonely, for she played with her animal friends every day. She sang to them, and told them about her dreams of falling in love.

Sixteen years went by, and no one discovered Aurora's secret home. Her only companions were the birds and fluffy-tailed squirrels and rabbits.

They disguised themselves as peasants and raised
Aurora deep in the woods. To be extra safe, the fairies
agreed to stop using magic so that no one – especially
Maleficent – would suspect them.

The king and queen were horrified. But the good fairies, Flora, Fauna and Merryweather, came up with a plan to protect Princess Aurora from Maleficent.

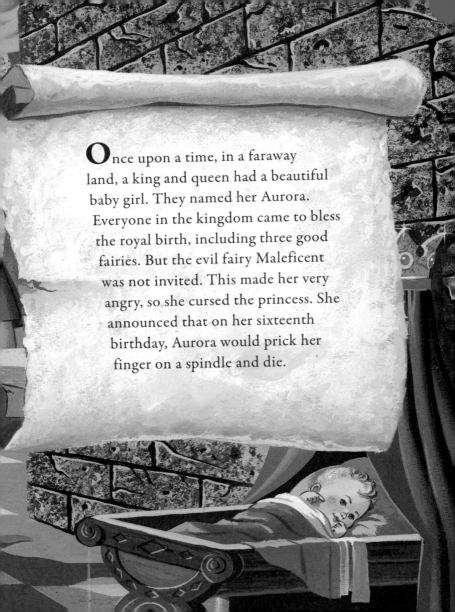

Once upon a time, in a faraway land, a king and queen had a beautiful baby girl. They named her Aurora. Everyone in the kingdom came to bless the royal birth, including three good fairies. But the evil fairy Maleficent was not invited. This made her very angry, so she cursed the princess. She announced that on her sixteenth birthday, Aurora would prick her finger on a spindle and die.

WALT DISNEY's
Sleeping Beauty

Story adapted by Monique Peterson

Pictures by The Walt Disney Studios
adapted by Norm McGary

One day a handsome prince came riding through
the forest. As soon as he saw Snow White, he fell in
love with her. Kneeling by her coffin, he kissed her.

Snow White sat up, blinked, and smiled.
True Love's Kiss had broken the spell.

As the Seven danced with joy, the Prince carried
Snow White off to his castle, where they lived
happily ever after.

But it was too late for Snow White. She was so
beautiful, even in death, that the Seven could not bear
to part with her. They built her a coffin of glass and
gold, and day and night they kept watch over their
beloved princess.

Told by the birds and animals that something was wrong, the Seven raced back to the cottage. They saw the Queen sneaking off, and they ran after her.

As storm clouds gathered and rain began to fall, the Seven chased the Queen to the top of a high, rocky mountain.

Crack! There was a flash of lightning, and the evil queen fell to her doom below.

A few minutes later, the Queen came to the
kitchen window.

"Making pies, dearie?" she asked. "It's apple pies
the men love. Here, taste one of these." She held
the poisoned apple out to Snow White.

Snow White remembered her friends' warning.
But the woman looked harmless, and the apple
looked delicious.

Snow White bit the apple. Then, with a sigh,
she fell to the floor.

The next morning before they left for the mine, the Seven warned Snow White to be on her guard.

"Don't let nobody or nothin' in the house," said Grumpy.

"Oh, Grumpy," said Snow White, "you *do* care! I'll be careful, I promise." She kissed him and the others good-bye, and the men went cheerfully off to work.

Meanwhile, the Queen had learned from her mirror that Snow White was still alive.

With a magic spell, she turned herself into an old peddler woman. She filled a basket with apples, putting a poisoned apple on top. "One bite," she cackled, "and Snow White will sleep forever. Then I'll be the fairest in the land!"

That night after supper, they all sang and
danced and made merry music. Bashful played the
concertina. Happy tapped the drums. Sleepy tooted
his horn. Grumpy played the organ. And Dopey
wiggled his ears!

Snow White loved her new friends. And she felt
safe at last.

When Snow White told her new friends about the Queen's plan to kill her, they decided that she should stay with them.

"We're askin' for trouble," huffed Grumpy.

"But we can't let her get caught by that kwicked ween – I mean, wicked queen!" said Doc. The others agreed.

Snow White woke with a start and saw the Seven gathered around her. "Why, you're not children," she said. "You're little men!"

"I read your names on the beds," she continued. "Let me guess who you are. You're Doc. And you're Bashful. You're Sleepy. You're Sneezy. And you're Happy and Dopey. And you must be Grumpy!"

The Seven were amazed to find their house
so clean. They were even more amazed when they
went upstairs and saw Snow White!

"It's a girl!" said Doc.

"She's beautiful," sighed Bashful.

"Aw!" said Grumpy. "She's going to be trouble!
Mark my words!"

Meanwhile, the Seven Men, who lived in
the cottage, were heading home from the mine,
where they worked.

But inside, the little tables and chairs were covered with dust, and the sink was filled with dirty dishes.

"My!" said Snow White. "Perhaps the children who live here are orphans and need someone to take care of them. Maybe they'll let me stay and keep house for them."

The animals all helped, and soon the place was neat and tidy.

At last Snow White fell wearily to the ground and
began to weep. The gentle animals of the forest gathered
around and tried to comfort her. Chirping and chattering,
they led her to a tiny cottage.

"Oh," said Snow White, "it's adorable! Just like
a doll's house."

Frightened, Snow White fled through the
woods. Branches tore at her clothes. Sharp twigs
scratched her arms and legs. Strange eyes stared
from the shadows. Danger lurked everywhere.
Snow White ran on and on.

"The Queen?" gasped Snow White.

"She's jealous of you," said the Huntsman. "She'll stop at nothing. Quick – run away and don't come back. I'll lie to the Queen. Now, go! Run! Hide!"

The next day Snow White, never suspecting that she was in danger, went off with the Huntsman.

When they were deep in the woods, the Huntsman drew his knife. Then, suddenly, he fell to his knees.

"I can't do it," he sobbed. "Forgive me." He told her it was the Queen who had ordered this wicked deed.

The Queen sent for her huntsman.

"Take Snow White deep into the forest," she said, "and there, my faithful huntsman, you will kill her."

The man begged the Queen to have mercy, but she would not be persuaded. "Silence!" she warned. "You know the penalty if you fail!"

One day when the Queen spoke to her mirror, it replied with the news she had been dreading. There was now someone even more beautiful than the Queen. And that person was Snow White!

Despite all the hard work, Snow White stayed
sweet, gentle and cheerful.

Day after day she washed and swept and
scrubbed. And day after day she dreamed of a
handsome prince who would come and carry her
off to his castle.

As time passed, Snow White grew more and more beautiful – and the Queen grew more and more envious. So she forced the princess to dress in rags and work from dawn to dusk.

The Queen had magic powers and owned a
wondrous mirror that spoke. Every day she stood
before it and asked:

"Magic Mirror on the wall,
Who is the fairest one of all?"
And every day the mirror answered:
"You are the fairest one of all, O Queen,
The fairest our eyes have ever seen."

Her stepmother, the Queen, was cruel and vain. She hated anyone whose beauty rivaled her own – and she watched her stepdaughter with angry, jealous eyes.